Otter B
BRAVE

WRITTEN BY
Pamela Kennedy & Anne Kennedy Brady

ILLUSTRATED BY
Aaron Zenz

TYNDALE

Tyndale House Publishers, Inc.
Carol Stream, Illinois

FOCUS ON THE FAMILY®

A Focus on the Family book published by Tyndale House Publishers, Inc.,
Carol Stream, Illinois 60188

Cover design by Josh Lewis
Cover illustration by Aaron Zenz

Book Design by Josh Lewis
Text set in Source Sans and Prater Sans Pro.

For manufacturing information regarding this product, please call
1-800-323-9400.

For information about special discounts for bulk purchases, please contact
Tyndale House Publishers at csresponse@tyndale.com, or call 1-800-323-9400.

Library of Congress Cataloging-in-Publication Data can be found at
www.loc.gov.

ISBN 978-1-58997-033-5

Printed in Malaysia

25   24   23   22   21   20   19
7   6   5   4   3   2   1

It was Show and Tell time in Otter B's class.
He and his friends gathered in a circle as
Ms. Woods called Felicia up to the front.
Felicia always brought something interesting
to share, and she was good at telling stories.
Otter B wiggled with excitement.

Felicia stood in front of the class
and zoomed her toy airplane over her head.

"My Aunt Francine is a pilot,
and she gave me this plane,"
Felicia explained.

"There's a red lightning bolt
on the tail. That's why I
named it Lightning."

She took a bow and everyone clapped.

Then Ms. Woods pulled a name from a hat.

"Tomorrow will be Otter B's turn to bring in something special and tell us about it!"

Otter B gulped. His tummy felt fluttery. His knees felt shaky.
"I don't want to do Show and Tell!" he whispered.

Roscoe leaned closer.
"Don't be shy, Otter B,"
he said. But Otter B
felt very shy.

Felicia swished her fluffy tail.
"I think talking in front
of the class is fun!"

It didn't sound fun to Otter B at all.

Tabitha pulled her head into her shell.
"You could pretend to be sick
tomorrow and stay home!"
she suggested.

But Otter B was pretty sure lying would
only make him feel worse.

On the way home from school, Otter B talked
to his best friend, Franklin.
"What if I forget what to say?"
Otter B buried his face in his paws.
"What if everyone laughs at me?"

Franklin thought for a moment.
"Well, it wouldn't be everyone," he said,
"because I would never laugh at my best friend."

Franklin winked, then hopped up to his house.

That night at dinner, Otter B told Mama and Daddy about Show and Tell. "I'm going to be all by myself up there, and everyone will stare at me!"

Daddy put down his fork. "You know," he said, "sometimes I feel nervous when I have to talk in front of people, too. Like when I give a presentation at work."

Otter B stared at Daddy. "You?"

Daddy smiled. "Sure! But God says He's always with me. Remembering that helps me feel brave."

Mama nodded. "That's right. And God also gives us friends to help us feel less afraid! Think of all the good friends in your class."

Otter B suddenly sat up straight.
"I have a great idea!" he announced.
"Can I please be excused?"

He sped off before Mama could even answer.
She and Daddy chuckled as they watched
him scamper to his room.

The next morning, when it was time for Show and Tell, Otter B grabbed Franklin's hand and pulled him up beside him!

"Hey, what's going on?" Franklin asked.
Otter B held up a picture he'd drawn the night before.

"My Show and Tell is a picture
of Franklin and me,"
he explained. Franklin blinked,
then beamed.

"He's a really good friend because he helps me and cares about how I feel. I brought him up here with me because I was scared to do Show and Tell alone. And Daddy told me God is always with me, too! So now I feel braver, because I don't have to do it all by myself."

Otter B and Franklin sat down, and nobody laughed at them. In fact, everyone clapped and cheered! It wasn't nearly as scary as Otter B had thought it would be.

Actually, it was so much fun that Otter B thought he might try being brave again.

If you are feeling nervous
and you're shaky in the knees,
try asking God to make you brave.
It's how you Otter Be!

Be strong and brave. Do not be afraid. Do not lose hope. I am the LORD your God. I will be with you everywhere you go.
Joshua 1:9